Lesson Plans:
An Education in Romance

Lainey Davis

Lesson Plans: An Education in Romance

By Lainey Davis

Join my newsletter and never miss a new release!

LaineyDavis.com

Many thanks to Nicky Lewis, Arwen Davis, and Elizabeth Perry for editorial input. Thank you to the nurses who read this work for authenticity and offered advice on Amy's journey!

Thank you for supporting independent authors!

She's totally off limits...and she's also kind of mean. He wants her anyway.

Doug Rogers has it all planned out. He just needs to teach summer school and one tiny class at the nearby university and his master's in education will be paid for. But he wasn't planning on Amy Peterson.

The almost-nurse in his comp class seems mad at the world, and particularly mad at Doug. She's one class away from her nursing degree after five long years of hard work, and she doesn't have the time or the patience for her optimistic instructor, no matter how attractive he is behind those glasses. The more he tries to talk to her, the more he seems to shove his foot in his mouth.

When a work accident brings Doug to the emergency room, he sees Amy in action and knows he's a goner for this fierce, competent woman. Except...she's still his student for another week.

Lesson Plans: An Education in Romance is a steamy prequel linking the Stag Brothers series and Bridges and Bitters. Readers have loved Doug and Amy from the sidelines. See how their story begins in this novella.

CHAPTER ONE

Doug

I never take selfies, but today feels special.

Plus, I can text this selfie to my mother, knowing she hates everything about my workplace. At some point, I'll stop taking joy in upsetting my parents. But today, I grin and extend my arm, positioning the camera so Franklin Middle School's gorgeous stone entryway frames my face.

Today was my last day of student teaching, which means tomorrow will be my first day getting paid to be here. Granted, I'm starting off in summer school, so I'm sure not making much. But as I told my family, teaching makes me happy.

Lord knows why. Just as I snap the picture I notice a group of pre-teens cheesing in the background, spoiling my shot. I whip my head around. "What are you two still doing here? Did you miss the bus?"

They snort. "Duh. Soccer practice."

I scowl and glance down the block toward the athletic field. "Well get over to practice, then. Mr. Nesso's probably looking for you."

Another snort as they start walking. "He probably don't even know we're gone."

"It's *doesn't*!" I holler at their backs, already feeling like their dorky English teacher. I chuckle when they flip me the bird, and try again for the selfie. This time, my smile feels more genuine.

"Mr. Rogers! May I speak with you?" The smile drops from my lips when I hear the principal, Kellie Vinelli, approaching. Perpetually perky, Ms. Vinelli ends every one of her sentences in an exclamation point. But she's also a keen observer and I feel like...well, I feel like I've been called to the principal's office.

I clear my throat. "Yes, ma'am."

She smiles. I clench my teeth. "Mr. Rogers, were you unclear about Colton's meaning just there?"

"Unclear?"

"I couldn't help but notice you corrected his grammar!"

I wince. "Well, I'm an English teacher."

"Yes, you are! In a diverse school where we focus on cultural competency!"

I sigh. She's reminding me how much more I still have to learn about this work. It feels like a strange thing to say since I came here to teach. "I'm still finding my feet," I tell her, fiddling in my pocket.

I grew up in a wealthy suburb where most people look the same and insist on the same sorts of values. I majored in business because my parents told me to, because they expected me to, because my brother did. I can admit that I first switched to education to spite them. It seemed like the best way to irritate my family, but still make sure I got some sort of job after college.

Once I started my education classes, though, I felt like I was in the right place for the first time in my life. I felt like I had a direction...a path that led to me goofing around with a bunch of pre-teens all day long.

Kellie smiles. "In your shoes, I might have reassured Colton that Mr. Nesso always knows who is and is not present!"

Nodding, I think about how hard it is to drill down to the important lesson in the moment. I focused on how Colton shaped his words rather than emphasize that his teachers here always care and always see him. I'm not sure what to say in response, so I'm grateful when Kellie Vinelli fills the silence. "I believe you'd better hurry if you're still meeting the graduate program director!"

The last time Kellie Vinelli called me in her office, she suggested I start right away on my master's degree. The district has a lot of incentives in place to snag new teachers and keep us. Ms. Vinelli wasted no time setting me up with some funding in exchange for a commitment to stay with the Public Schools of Pittsburgh. Of course, this means I'll be teaching summer school, taking my own summer classes, and teaching one course for the university to pay for it.

I slap my pocket, where her signed forms are still nestled. "Thanks for the reminder." I give her a grin and jog off for the bus toward campus.

She waves me off as I climb aboard. "See you Monday!"

I arrive at the health sciences building with about ten minutes to spare, but there's a student in the office already, so I lean against the wall in the hall staring at the photos of nursing students and lab researchers. I hear the scrape of a chair against the floor in the office.

"You truly can't cut me a break with this?" A female voice sounds agitated. "I've been doing the work for this degree for years. I just need a freaking piece of paper." I hear the woman make a gasping sound, like one of those almost-crying hiccups.

The department chair clears his throat. "Ms. Peterson, in order for me to give you the 'piece of paper' as you call it, you're going to need to complete your first-year composition course. There is no work-around for this requirement."

I clench my teeth. Things sound heated in there as the female voice scoffs. "I've been charting vitals...I've read so many charts from the RN's. Do I really need to do book reports to get the job done?"

"Ms. Peterson, I'm sorry. Rules are rules. You can take the composition course during the summer session and still finish your degree for August graduation."

The student's response is softer now, muffled. I realize I'm leaning closer to the door to eavesdrop and pull myself together as the door flies inward. My eyes bulge out of my head a little when I see an enraged woman wearing blue scrubs storming out of the door in a blur of brown ponytail and tote bags.

She's hot. I don't just mean her temper. I mean, she's attractive as hell. For some reason, the rage really does it for me. The paper flyers taped to the walls flutter in the hallway as she streaks out of the building, and I have to take a deep breath to calm myself down.

"Ah, Mr. Rogers, come in, come in." I whip my head back toward the open office door, where Professor Blee is seated behind a mountain of file folders.

"Doug, please," I say, pulling out my signed forms and taking a seat in the folding chair vacated by that hurricane of a woman. It's still warm from her ass. Lord help me, I need to focus on this meeting. "I just stopped by to drop off the last forms for the teaching assistant gig."

Professor Blee nods his head, reaching for the paper. "Forgive me. Your folder is somewhere in here." He gestures at the pile. "I'll hunt for it while you tell me what you need to know in order to hit the ground running for the summer session."

He begins sifting through the manila folders as I stare at him. "Um, everything? Like...well...everything."

Professor Blee looks up and raises his eyebrows. "Were you not teaching English and Composition to middle schoolers for your student teaching assignment?" I nod. He smiles. "Well, then! You're all set." In response to my confused expression he waves a hand. "You're teaching first-year comp to nursing students, Mr. Rogers. Unlike most students at this university, they know exactly what they want to do upon graduation and they know exactly what that job entails." He holds up a folder triumphantly and shakes it around, sliding my signed forms inside. "Many of our teaching assistants find it useful to tap into our syllabus directory. We don't have a required textbook, but many choose to use...this one." He extracts a book from the mountain on his desk and shoves it toward me.

Then he turns to his computer as if I'm no longer in the room. I clutch the book to my chest as he types and then peers at me, confused. "Was there something else?"

I shake my head, understanding a little better why that woman got so heated in here.

I cram the textbook in my shoulder bag and catch a bus toward home. A few blocks later, I see the angry woman from before, her ponytail swishing behind her as she storms up the sidewalk. She's definitely still cute, despite the rage seeping out of her. Even through the crusty bus window I can see that she's exactly my type: stubborn, determined, fiery. The bus turns just as I start to wonder if she's a biter in bed. Ah, well. It's better that I didn't get a chance to make a move. I'm not going to have time for anything other than work this summer.

CHAPTER TWO

Amy

One class left and I'll be a real nurse.

Just one class.

I feel like an old lady compared to the other students, though. Five years shouldn't make such a difference. It's not like I'm 30 in a room full of teenagers. But I'm not just any 23-year-old in freshmen comp. I already work full time as an emergency room tech and I already held my mom's hand as she died from cancer. I am not what you'd call a *peer* to these kids.

I find a seat in the back of the classroom, kick my bag under my seat and wonder how I'm supposed to swing eight hours a week of summer school in between my 12-hour shifts at work.

My boss offered to work around my schedule, but the reality is that I can't just walk off the floor if I'm elbows-deep inside a trauma patient's chest wound. The other students in class must be able to sense my resentment at being here, because they leave a ring of chairs open around me like a buffer zone. Half of them already failed freshmen comp the first time around and are trying to make it up before they end up like me—years too old to be steaming in a summer classroom.

I pull out what's left of my laptop. The lid creaks as I open it and I feel my cheeks flush, not wanting anyone to see the cracked screen. My brother Ryan didn't mean to drop it on the tile floor. I know that, but it doesn't change the fact that he did and we can't afford to replace it. Even with all of us living at home and pitching in, Dad can barely keep the house. Mom's treatments totally wiped out their savings and dug Dad into a deep financial hole. I can limp along with this clunker until I get my degree. It's just a few weeks. "I'll sleep when I'm old," I mutter as the teacher shuffles in.

He immediately walks to the white board and starts scratching out his name. I roll my eyes because his handwriting is worse than half the doctors I work with, and they at least have an excuse to be in a hurry. *DOUG ROGERS*, he scrawls. It's a douchey name, Doug.

I vow to think of him only as Doogie as he turns and uses his index finger to shove his glasses up his nose. I squint at him, because he looks familiar, but then he starts talking and I zone out.

Blah, blah, the syllabus is posted already. Blah, blah, we'll write an essay a week. He abruptly stops talking and I stare at him. His eyes widen and he hesitates before rattling off more course policies. I rest my chin on my fist and try not to fall asleep. I worked from seven until four and barely crammed food into my face before this class. I hope he doesn't keep us the entire two hours. Doogie holds up a spiral-bound bundle of papers. "Good news," he says. "Instead of a textbook, we'll be using this collection of essays I put together just for this class. You can pick this up at the campus bookstore." All around me, my classmates are popping gum and taking notes. I sit up, waiting for someone to point out that a custom print bundle means no ability to buy the book used or check it out from the university library. Nobody raises their hand.

I sigh and do it myself. Doogie's face lights up, and then his cheeks twitch, like he's not sure what expression to make. "Yes. You in the back. Question?"

"Amy Peterson," I mumble. "Did it occur to you that your custom bundle is the most expensive option for course materials?"

He frowns and looks down at the bundle. "It's significantly cheaper than the standard first-year comp book most of the other classes used."

I roll my eyes at him. "Yeah, new. But most of the other classes use it...so it's easy to get a used one cheap." Doogie presses his lips together and frowns. I tap my nails on the desk, waiting to see what he's going to say. I'm not sure what he could say at this point. He obviously already ordered the copies. There's no going back now. Maybe I'm waiting for him to apologize. I don't even know anymore.

Eventually he clears his throat. "I had not considered the resale value of the other textbooks, no, Ms. Peterson." He's quiet for a beat and then continues. "But, as I said, this is a customized book just for this course." He smiles and looks around the room. "I think you'll find the readings align with your interests as future nurses!" My classmates perk up and Doofus Rogers turns back to the board, writing out some nonsense with a squeaky marker.

I was irritated at being here to begin with and this is not helping. I felt like such a failure when I had to drop this class as an actual freshman. I know my mom would scold me for that attitude, and she'd want me to take a deep breath and move on. *It's just one class, Amy-girl,* she'd say.

I feel tears start welling when I think of my mom, when I think of how different my life is after her illness and death. I try to focus on the teacher, but my mood is darker than before.

He asks us all to hand-write a few hundred words for him about what we expect to gain from this class and to tell him the last significant piece of writing we completed. My stomach growls audibly and I rest a hand on my belly as I begin to scratch out my temper in my spiral notebook.

I'm in this class to complete my final requirement for my BSN. That's what I hope to gain. The last thing of significance that I wrote was an email to my employer, explaining that I once again could not meet the requirements for advancement because I still haven't completed my first-year composition class. And on I vent for a few paragraphs.

I scribble my name at the top of the page and noisily rip it out of my notebook. When Doogie collects the papers, he dismisses us for a five-minute break. I walk out of the room, out of the building, and into the humid June air. I feel tears start welling and I know I can't go back in there. Not today. Maybe I'm too tired from work. Maybe I'm just hungry. But I don't have it in me to finish this class tonight. I cross Fifth Ave and hop aboard the 71B bus toward home, knowing I probably fucked myself over already, but too exhausted to care.

I walk in the door to a wreck, which I expected. Dad and Ryan are asleep on the couch with the baseball game blaring on the television. Judging by the noise, my brother Dan is up in his room raging against a machine. And of course my baby sister, Alice, is trying to clean up. Her curly hair stands up all over the place as she furiously scrubs at a pan of something.

I shake my head as I set my bag down on the floor, worried the towering stack of dishes is going to crash down on Alice. "Why isn't anyone helping you with that?" I chide, hurrying to grab a towel and make some headway on the already-washed pans so we've got some room to stack clean plates. "What happened to not having to wash up if you're the one who cooks?"

Alice blows her hair out of her eyes and shrugs. She doesn't have to tell me that Dad's not the greatest at implementing systems to keep the house going. In the years since Mom died, I've been fully in charge of operations around here, but with me working full time and going to school as well...

I stalk over to the couch with my damp dish towel and whip it at Ryan's face. His eyes fly open and he swats his arms in the air. "What gives? Oh. It's you." He crosses his arms over his chest and tries to fall back asleep, but I whip him with the towel again, this time catching him right on the eyelid.

"Ha!" I shout triumphantly as he flies off the couch, ready to fight. I shake my head. "You and Dan should be washing up. I'm sure you two didn't make dinner..."

He groans. "It didn't even taste good. Beans and some green shit."

"Watch your mouth." Dad mutters in his sleep from the corner of the couch. Ryan sighs and walks to the sink, where Alice happily steps aside. My stomach gurgles and Alice's face lights up.

"I'll fix you a plate!" She's in motion before I can protest and I sink into a stool at the counter, waiting for her to pull something amazing out of the microwave. Alice has aspirations of being a chef. She just finished up the culinary arts program at the high school vo-tech, but there's no money for her to go to culinary school for real.

I try not to think about all my siblings' dreams on hold. At least Dan and Ry were able to leave high school with industry certifications from their tech programs. They both chip in a lot from their jobs. I'll be making almost twice as much as I am now, once I get this damned degree. The hospital is as eager to hire me as a nurse as I'm eager to get the job. Things will improve.

My sister sets a steaming plate of food in front of me on the counter and I dig in. "Al, this tastes amazing." She doesn't have to tell me she made beans and greens because they're cheap. "What'd you do to get all this flavor?"

Alice leans forward on her elbows, beaming. "I got a bunch of bones from the meat counter to make the broth. No charge! And I splurged on a few different kinds of onions."

"Onions are a splurge?" I wince, knowing the biggest expense right now is my tuition. I'm sure the stupid packet for my comp class will put us even deeper in the hole. If I'm still allowed in the class.

Reading my face, Alice sits beside me. "You're home earlier than I thought. How was school?"

"Shouldn't I be asking you that question?"

Alice giggles. "Aim, it's June! You're the only nerd in summer school."

There's a clatter from the sink and Ryan groans as bean-covered dishes slide into the water, splashing him. Alice and I laugh before we head over to help dig him out of trouble. I remind myself this is why I'm working myself ragged for the degree.

This family right here is all I have, and we stick together. I can deal with Doogie the Douche for a few weeks. I shovel the last bite of my dinner into my mouth and rinse my dish. I walk back into the living room and kiss my dad on the cheek. "I'm heading up," I tell them. Dad grunts as I turn down the volume on the game. I kick Dan's door as I pass and he turns the volume down just in time for me to sink into bed. I'm asleep before I can even resume worrying about everything.

CHAPTER THREE

Doug

I don't know what to make of Amy Peterson being my student, and I'm a little shaken to realize I'm nervous to read her essay. I just...wasn't expecting my students to be real, complex people. The rest of the class wrote hopefully about their collegiate dreams; about how they enjoyed their first year away from home. "The city is so big!" "It's been so great living on my own in the dorms." I expected that sort of thing.

I think back to Amy pointing out the cost of the packet and I cringe. Kellie Vinelli's reminder about cultural competency echoes through my mind. How can I be so consistently unaware of where my students are coming from? I should know more about the hidden costs of education by now. I thought I was being the cool T.A., picking out a series of essays about healthcare rather than assigning a textbook.

I check my watch. I'm supposed to offer office hours for students to come meet with me to talk about upcoming assignments or get help with their papers. So far nobody has shown up. It gives me time to grade their drafts before I head home for the night, so at least there's that. "Hm." Amy's paper sits on the top of the stack, the last one to grade.

It took me a full minute to recover when I realized the sexy, angry woman from my boss's office is in fact my student. And then it took a lot of conscious effort to stop thinking of her as sexy once she continued to be fiery in class...until she stormed out during the break, that is.

At least she turned in her paper first.

Technically she met the barest of minimum requirements for the assignment. She didn't elaborate on anything here, but the whole goal of the exercise was for me to get a sense of where the students are in terms of their ability to string sentences together. Amy Peterson certainly knows how to do that.

I write a B on top of the sheet and tuck everything into my bag, wondering if she will show up for class today, or if I should penalize her for leaving early on the first night of class. I recall from that day in

Professor Blee's office that she's one class away from graduating. She's what the department calls a "nontraditional" student since she's older than her peers in the course.

I shake my head rapidly, trying to stop myself from cataloging all the nontraditional aspects of Amy Peterson. It seems really unfair that I should meet a woman, find her this attractive, and then be utterly forbidden from doing anything about it.

I decide to make a note of Amy leaving early but not to do anything else about it at this point. It's not like I remembered to include the attendance policy paragraph I was supposed to add to my syllabus. I really need to reach out to some of the other grad students to get some pointers. I'm flying blind over here.

When I get to my classroom, Amy is seated in the back with her arms crossed over her chest. She's silent through the entire discussion of what makes a good introductory paragraph. I'm feeling pretty good as I realize there are a lot of similarities between this subject matter and what I teach at the middle school. I can go into more depth with these students, but Amy isn't interested in depth. She's silent when I ask the class for input on the essay I assigned them to read for homework, but when I ask the students to discuss the work with a partner, I notice that she contributes to the conversation. Can it be possible that she's shy? It feels ridiculous to wonder if her hesitation is due to her liking me as much as I like her.

By the fourth night of class, I realize in horror that I'm staring at Amy's—at my student's—nipples as they harden in her scrub top as she sits in the frigid classroom, listening to a peer read aloud from her essay draft.

I close my eyes and blow out a slow breath. This is not good. I drag a hand down my cheek and check my watch. It's late. I must be exhausted and hungry, I rationalize. "Hey, class, try and wrap up your conversation. Essays are due to me via email by nine in the morning, so I'll let you go a little early to work on them at home."

There's a chorus of celebration and the students file out of the room quickly. I move to pack up my notes and startle when I see that Amy is still in the room, biting her lip as she furiously writes something down in her notebook.

I clear my throat. "Did you need something, Ms. Peterson?" I realize I'm hoping she says yes, that she'll say she needs me to lean over her and explain paragraphing nice and slow. *Oh god, I'm such a creep.*

Amy shakes her head. "Just finishing up." She sighs and looks around. "Do you know which computer labs are still open on campus?"

I furrow my brow. "I have no idea."

Amy scoffs. "Well, thanks for all the help." She rolls her eyes at me and rips a sheet from her notebook. She slaps it against my chest as she walks past. "That'll have to do for my submission. My computer finally fucking died and I have to catch a bus."

I stare at the paper, knowing I shouldn't allow a student to speak to me like this, but not sure how to intervene. Hell, this is the first time I considered that not all of my students have access to a computer. By the time I recover from my shock, she's gone into the night.

I should have offered to look up the lab schedules or something. I should have done anything else. Instead I'm remembering the instant her skin pressed against mine, the warmth of her palm even through paper and my cotton shirt.

I read through Amy's paper and see she's written a perfectly serviceable introduction, summarized her argument and transitioned nicely into her first paragraph. But it's well under the length requirement and—it should go without saying even inside my own head—it's not typed.

I sit at my desk and try to figure out why it bothers me so much that I'm going to have to give Amy Peterson a poor grade for her assignment. I think back to one of Kellie Vinelli's perky memos, where she wrote *We cannot shy away from letting students experience consequences for their choices!*

The phrase stuck with me because it seemed to apply to so many aspects of my life. My parents think I'm going to experience negative consequences from my choice to abandon the uppity lifestyle my extended family pretends to relish. So far the consequences have been pretty freeing...

The stakes are different for Amy Peterson, though. I don't like being in this position. I also feel like I learned something today about requiring typed work and the impact that could have on my students. I sigh and award her a B, making a note in the margin about the summer hours for the computer lab.

She doesn't show up for class the next day to collect her paper.

CHAPTER FOUR

Amy

I don't know what the hell I'm thinking. Well. I know what I'm thinking. It's just not okay.

I fell asleep last night dreaming about my instructor. In my dream, he grabbed my hand when I pressed my essay paper to his chest. He pulled me close and told me I was a naughty girl. I woke up sweating just as dream-Doogie was about to spank me.

So how did I respond? By skipping class. I'm putting my entire family's sacrifices at risk, fucking up, and missing class.

I hate that I'm already a bitter, shrewish person at the ripe old age of 23. What am I even doing with my life? Snapping at people...mentally calling my professor Doogie just for doing his job.

I need to get over this little crush. I don't have time for a hot teacher fantasy. I need to finish my course and get my degree. But when an ambulance rolls into the bay toward the end of my shift, I can't just walk out while a trauma patient hemorrhages. By the time we get everything under control, I've missed an hour of class.

I could go for the last half. I could take Doogie aside afterward and explain—beg him to excuse my lateness.

I opt to go home and shower.

I'm not surprised when I open my email on my phone and see a message from Doogie.

Ms. Peterson: Can you come to my office hours next week to talk about your progress in my course? You are at risk of failure given your number of absences.

—Doug

Risk of failure.

Tears well up in my eyes as I stare at the message. I hear my brothers blasting loud music in their rooms below mine. Dad let me have the entire third floor since I'm the oldest and I carry the heaviest load around here. How long will that be true? Do I seriously want to keep working at the lower wages of an ER tech when I'm this close to my goals?

I wipe my eyes with the back of my hand and try to find the syllabus Doogie handed out on the first day of class. I've never been to office hours a day in my life. It's not like the material is difficult for me. I even begrudgingly enjoy reading the stupid essays he picked out about how fucked up it is that nurses in this country are treating so many patients at once—the ratios are apparently worse at other hospitals in the country.

I hate that this guy apparently knows about these issues, at least enough to find something for us to read about them. It just makes him hotter. I sigh and fire off a response.

Professor Rogers: I work during your office hours.

—Amy

My phone flashes with an immediate reply.

Ms. Peterson: Please, call me Doug. I'm just a grad student...what's your schedule like? I can be flexible.

—Doug

I guess I'm chatting with my professor now, over email. Which is a thought I should strike from my head immediately, because he's the person standing between my nursing career and a big, fat failure.

Doug: I'm pretty much only free on weekend afternoons. Which is when I planned to do the actual work for your class.

—Amy Peterson, almost RN

Amy: Saturday is a great day to meet at the library! Hardly any teenagers around, nobody making noise...plus I can help you with your work for my class.

I bite my cheek, laughing a little about his teenager joke even as I bang on the floor when my teenaged brother turns the music back up.

No offense, but I don't need "help" with your class...I just need <u>time</u> to read the essays about nursing shortages, etc.

My heart flutters at the next ping of my email app. I feel like a teenager myself right now. But I still open the message immediately, greedily.

How about this? We'll meet, we'll talk about attendance, and then we can both just do our work in silence. See you Saturday.

The message comes with a weird attachment that, when I click it, opens my calendar app. He's pretty slick with the technology.

I don't hate it.

I can't decide if it's creepy that he's offering to meet me on a Saturday afternoon at the university library. I guess graduate students aren't like regular people who clock out on a Friday and spend the weekend watching baseball like my brothers and Dad.

There's no way in hell I'll be able to concentrate on my reading sitting next to Doug at a table in the library. God, he'd probably roll up his shirt sleeves halfway. I move closer to the box fan in my window, suddenly uncomfortably hot.

I accept Doug's invite and go to bed.

CHAPTER FIVE

Doug

When I see the email that my summer school colleagues are going to try their hand at pickleball in the park on Saturday, I'm tempted to bail so I can focus on grading and reading for my own courses. But I'm feeling pretty starved for companionship right now after a long week of teaching and doing grad school work. Whacking balls sounds pretty tempting, and I hitch a ride with a pair of history teachers who live close by.

I've never played pickleball before, but I assume it's close enough to tennis that I won't embarrass myself. Thinking about tennis sends me right back to private lessons my family pushed on me to prepare me for the rigors of elite boarding school. I shake away those memories and hope I do all right on the court today.

I stand on the curb waiting for Jay and Phil to swing by and grab me. I hop in the back seat of Jay's sedan when he slides to a stop. "Man," I say as I climb in. I find I'm comforted by Jay clearly being able to afford a nice, dependable-yet-responsible car. "You can barely hear these hybrid cars approach. This is pretty quiet."

He nods. "Yeah, it's a sweet ride. I might get one of those all electric cars once this guy dies off. You need to borrow a paddle?"

He elbows Phil, who holds up a bouquet of neon paddles, grinning. "I do indeed need to borrow one," I tell him. "You guys have your own set?"

Phil shrugs. "They come in a four-pack. Newman's meeting us up there. He called dibs on the orange one already." We park near the courts and wave at Newman Nesso, our middle school gym teacher, who is holding on to a net on the end of an entire sea of pickleball courts. Newman is on the short side with calves the size of cantaloupes and looks exactly like a middle school gym teacher, especially when he wears polo shirts year round.

I wonder what led him to be friends with Jay and Phil, who both wear glasses like me and, like me, have the pale skin bookworms cultivate in libraries. We make an unlikely foursome, but they create a friendly atmosphere and it doesn't take me long to relax.

"I had no idea all this was up here." I set my water bottle to the side and bounce the ball a few times, enjoying the thwop sound it makes.

Newman dances around, stretching and kicking like he's setting up for the Olympics. I briefly wonder if pickleball is an Olympic sport when he points his orange paddle at me. "Rogers, you with me?" I shrug. "Awesome. Winner buys the first round. And I hate spending money."

Soon, we're exchanging volleys with Jay and Phil like we've been doing this for years. And honestly? It feels great. There's no pretense, nobody sneaking in sly jabs about anybody's family background. Sure, Newman's wearing sweatbands and acting like Andy Roddick if we miss a ball, but we can all tell he's mostly kidding.

I love that all these guys are teaching summer school, mostly because they care about the kids who need the program rather than because they need the extra cash. I feel an ease around them I never felt in my hometown growing up—like I've really found my people, even if they're a little bit strange.

We play for a few hours and then relocate to a bar with outdoor seating, sipping cheap, lite beer in the sun and talking about our students. Newman spins his paddle around on his knee and grins, shaking his head. "I'd love to get the kids up to the park to play one day. Think we could have them walk? The bus is the only expensive part."

Jay frowns, considering. "It's like two miles, mostly uphill from the school. I don't think they'd be into it."

We all sigh. A thought occurs to me as I sip my drink. "What about playing indoors with them, though? In the gym? We could tape out a court...maybe use the volleyball nets?"

Phil shakes his head. "Gym's booked all summer for sports camps." He makes the gesture for money with both hands, signaling the school's for-profit rental venture.

Newman bangs the racket off the edge of the table. "Ah, well. What can I actually have them do for summer school phys-ed that's not some variation of sharks and minnows?"

We brainstorm ideas with him until I'm actually looking forward to partnering up for a walking field trip to a nearby park to launch different sized toy cars off the slide. "You can team teach with someone from science, and I'll get them through the lab reports afterward," I suggest.

Newman's face lights up and he clinks his plastic beer cup against mine. "I like how you think, Rogers."

"Call me Doug, man. Rogers is my dad."

He laughs and shakes his head. "My dad would never have team taught. I can tell you that much."

My eyebrows fly up. "He hates teachers, too?"

My friends make shocked expressions. Newman shakes a head. "No, dude. My dad taught science for this school district for 25 years. He just wouldn't have ever collaborated."

Jay frowns and pours the last beer from the pitcher on the table. "Your dad hates teachers?"

I look around the table at the group of men I sort of assumed were all like me, passionate about education but also bucking years of family tradition to make it a reality. "Um, yes. My family thinks I'm a traitor to our legacy or some shit."

"I'm sorry to hear that." Phil claps me on the back and points around the table. "I think most of the summer school crew is at least second gen teachers."

"Seriously? That's pretty cool."

We talk about how in all of their families, they showed their rebellious streak by entering a different subject matter of expertise than their parents. "I had no idea there were whole family traditions like this." I shake my head. "It must be amazing to grow up with people who enjoy doing things for others."

That gets a laugh and Phil signals the server to bring us another pitcher. I'm feeling pretty good, physically tired and a little buzzed. Once Phil pours out another round of drinks, he says, "My family went kind of ballistic when my sister bucked the trend to become a nurse."

At the word nurse, I freeze, a slosh of beer spilling onto my shirt. Shit. Amy. "Fuck," I mumble, flying to my feet and reaching around in my shorts to find my wallet. I slap a few bills on the table and look at my watch. There's no way she's still waiting. "I was supposed to meet one of my undergrads at the library."

I pat myself down, locating my cell phone. I wave at the guys and tear off toward the university on foot. At every red light, I skitter across the street anyway, wincing at the thought of letting down Amy Peterson, the one person who couldn't afford to waste time. I feel my heart race at the thought of her angry expression and realize I don't like being on her bad side. And then I shake my head.

She's a student. I shouldn't be thinking about her "sides" at all, should I? Amy Peterson might be older than my other students...but that doesn't make it any more wrong that I'm thinking about our email exchange, anticipating the look on her face when she tells me to fuck off. I don't have access to her phone number to reach out.

By the time I reach the library building, I'm sweating and panting, and the security guard makes a face. I roam through the entire first floor, shivering in the air conditioning, until I see her. I'm drawn to her, standing in a beam of light from the narrow windows near the wooden tables.

"Amy." Her name is a whisper and a shout at once and I rush to apologize for keeping her waiting. Before I can catch my breath I realize she is apologizing, too.

I laugh at the folly of it all, and I shiver a bit in the cool air. I notice she has goosebumps on her forearms and I reach my hand out to touch her skin, halting it in mid-air before I make contact. "Do you want to sit outside?" I shrug and gesture around the space. "It's too cold in here for me."

Amy sinks into the grass beneath a tree outside the library. She leans wearily against the trunk and I debate whether I should sit next to her. I decide against it and try not to man-spread in the grass while she pulls out her notebook. "I honestly have no idea what I'm doing," she mutters, whipping through the battered spiral-bound papers.

"Your writing is really quite good," I counter. "And from what I've overheard you seem to enjoy the readings in class."

She furrows her brow and looks at me like I'm an idiot. "I didn't mean with the classwork. I meant..." She sighs. "I keep missing your class and being rude to you and I don't know why." She rips out a hunk of grass and throws it to the side. "I'm just mad at the world right now. And I'm taking it out on you."

I chew on the inside of my cheek, gazing across the street at the hoards of people milling around the park plaza, seemingly without a care in the world. Amy Peterson's tough shell is like that damn scrub top today: thin and clingy enough for me to see the prickly bits. "I appreciate that you're honest about things like that. Not everyone has that, you know." She arches a brow at me. I never could arch a single brow. It's sexy and I close my eyes to stop the flood of attraction. "I just mean it's a rare thing, to be your real self with people. Even if your real self isn't shiny, happy perfection."

When I open my eyes, she's grinning at me. "So I'm not perfect? I'm what—dull?"

"God, that's not—" I rake a hand through my hair, ready to backpedal but Amy tips over in the grass laughing. She clasps her hands on her stomach and laughs and I exhale a deep breath.

She finally calms down and sits back up, bits of grass and dandelion fluff clinging to her long hair. She sighs. "Okay, Teach. You got me at office hours. Lay it on me."

I scoot closer to the tree and lean forward, my elbows on my knees. "You've got to come to class. That's the main thing here. I have to ding you for attendance."

"I will try my best to come to class."

I nod. "And you owe me a paper about the health insurance article."

She frowns. "Where did you come up with all those articles, anyway?"

Startled by the question, I lean back and shrug. "I tried to think about what my students would be interested in reading about. I really didn't want the class to be boring."

She reaches out a hand and presses it against my knee. I stare at her hand, firm on my skin. "It's definitely not boring."

My smile for her is genuine. I meet her eyes and forget that she's a student, that I'm a teaching assistant. I realize we're the same age, and I wish we'd met under different circumstances. "Thank you for the ringing endorsement."

She pulls back her hand and sighs, checking her watch. "I gotta get home."

For the first time, I wish I had a car so I could offer her a ride. I imagine what it would be like to pull up outside her house, lean across the console, wrap a hand around the back of her neck, ease her head close to mine and kiss the hell out of her. Maybe she'd yell at me. Maybe she'd say something almost nice. "See you in class, Amy."

"Thanks, Doug." She gathers her bags and stands, using the back of her forearm to brush her hair back from her face. "For everything."

CHAPTER SIX

Doug

Of course, Amy isn't in class Monday evening. I realize, maybe for the first time, the similarity between college students like Amy and the middle school students attending Franklin Middle School. I spend my days teaching kids who are balancing on a razor blade. Their families have no wiggle room, no cushion. One unexpected bill could land them in a shelter.

I get the sense that things are that precarious with Amy. She's certainly not in college on a scholarship and she definitely doesn't have family money paving her way. I hate that I might be a contributing factor to her not finishing her degree. Obviously I want all my students to think my class is important, but I can also see Amy's point...she should have taken the class five years ago and didn't. Now it just feels like busywork.

I sigh and teach the class all about transition sentences for a few hours. Once I send everyone home, I sit down to write Amy an email. I pull up the thread of our messages, wincing when I remember how excited I felt initially, seeing her name pop up on my phone. Reading her snarky replies. Like this woman gives zero fucks that I'm someone she should probably speak to a little more reverently.

Amy, I noticed you were not in class this evening. I want to do all I can to ensure you pass this course. Work with me, here...

Doug

I don't actually know how any of this works, how much leniency I can give her. I'm only in this role temporarily before I move to spend my days with middle schoolers. It seems more important to invest my time figuring out the power dynamics between teachers and students in that role. I go ahead and click send and hurry to catch the bus home.

The next day, Newman bursts into the teachers' lounge with an arm full of t-shirts. "You're not gonna believe what happened to me last night." He passes out a shirt to everyone and plops the rest of the stack on the table. I shake mine open to read the white lettering across the bright red cotton.

"Edgar Steiner's Pickle Pals?" Jay furrows his brow as he reads over my shoulder. "Newman, what the hell?"

Newman bounces on his toes as he slips the shirt over his head. "Edgar Steiner. The lawyer guy from TV? He was in line behind me at the grocery store yesterday."

"Edgar Steiner does his own shopping?" The guy's face is all over bus shelters and billboards, advertising his legal advice for anyone who's been in an accident.

Newman shrugs. "He was yesterday. And I was telling him about work, how I want to take the kids to the pickle ball courts but there's no money for bussing."

"How the hell long was that line?" Phil shakes his head as Newman presses a shirt toward him.

Newman is undeterred and slides the shirt over Phil's head as Phil squirms. "It was rush hour. Anyway! Edgar said he'd sponsor a bus. I already talked to Kellie Vinelli. The city has paddles and balls to lend. We just need to show up!"

I stare at the pile of shirts as more confused faculty trickle into the teachers' lounge. "Wait. We're just going to take them today? Just like that?"

Newman shrugs. "They all got field trip permission forms signed when they registered for summer school. Whenever we walk up the street to the library, that's technically a field trip." He claps his hands. "Pickle ball tourney, guys! All day!"

Before I can consider how this impacts my lesson plans, Newman has jumped into action, hauling crates of bagged lunches from the cafeteria and redirecting students to the street, where a fleet of yellow buses sits waiting to drive them a few miles to the park.

The whole thing feels a little ridiculous, but the kids seem to love that aspect of this unexpected diversion. They especially like that Newman has worked the staff into the roster for his tournament. Within the hour, fifty of the summer school kids and teachers are thwacking paddles in the sun and all of us are laughing. Our principal even blasts a not-terrible playlist from her phone through a speaker she brought from the school store.

Pickle Pals is just corny enough of a name that the teens feel comfortable teasing us about it, and I love the back and forth as we sit down for lunch in the shade near the courts. The school lunches aren't terrible—everyone gets a deli sandwich and an apple, although the milk cartons don't seem appetizing in the heat. I'd say it's a perfect day ... until Colton passes out when he goes to serve.

"Shit," Newman shouts, rushing over to the fallen seventh grader, who struggles to get back to his feet even as I urge him to stay down. Soon, we are swarmed with concerned teens and I stand up to widen the circle as Newman tries to get Colton to drink some water.

Kellie Vinelli, normally the perkiest person I've ever seen, has her phone out and I gather she's calling the paramedics. She places a hand over the phone and asks, "Does anyone have contact information for Colton's grown-ups?"

Newman's eyes widen. "I left the binder in the teachers' lounge," he says. "I got distracted with the lunch crates..."

Colton pushes up on to his elbows. "My ma's out of town for work this week and my grandma don't drive." He groans.

I feel the urge to correct his grammar and I'm proud of myself when I tamp that down and squeeze Colton's hand. "Doesn't your grandma have a phone, though? Can we call her to let her know we called the paramedics?"

Colton turns paler than before. "Mr. Rogers? We don't have insurance. I can't see—"

I hold up a hand. "Hey, buddy, you don't need to worry about that right now, okay?" Honestly, I'm not entirely sure how all that works, but I vow to figure it out for him. Paying for care never even crossed my mind growing up, and it's sitting at the top of Colton's priorities, above his worries about his health. Kids shouldn't have to worry about whether their families can afford to save their lives in a medical emergency. I hear Kellie Vinelli directing the ambulance crew up to the pickleball courts and I give Colton's shoulder a squeeze. "We're just going to make sure you're okay."

The paramedics arrive and ask him a series of questions. All signs point to heat stroke, but because this happened on our watch, our principal insists that Colton get checked out at the hospital. "Who's going to ride in with Mr. Bell?" She looks around at the staff, all engaged in calming down concerned teens they've corralled on the bleachers and out of the way.

"I'll go," I say. I'm already squatting on the ground next to Colton, who cringes as the paramedic attempts to start an IV. Colton looks up at me, his eyes unfocused, and I swallow. I've never had a student with a medical emergency before.

The paramedics load Colton onto the stretcher and start rolling him to the ambulance. I hear them talking about Colton's rapid pulse and high temperature and I remember that none of us were drinking our milk with our lunch. Was Colton taking breaks for water? I'm hot and thirsty myself, but it doesn't feel right to mention that. God, we should have been insisting they all stop for water periodically.

The ambulance heads for the closest emergency department rather than trekking across town to the children's hospital, and I'm blown away by how quickly they get Colton from the back of the ambulance into one of the treatment rooms. In the blink of an eye, the dark blue uniforms of the paramedics are replaced with the pale blue scrubs of hospital personnel.

I stand pressed against the wall, listening to words like "tachycardia" get thrown around as people roll in IV carts and trays of supplies. And then I see that one of the people helping Colton is Amy Peterson.

She crams a blood pressure cuff on his arm and one of those pulse checkers on his finger. She frowns at the numbers she sees on the machines. My jaw hangs open as I watch her squeeze his hand, look into his eyes, and assure him he's going to be just fine. "I know you're feeling lousy right now, bud," she says. "Your body stopped sweating, so I'm going to get you comfortable." He swallows and nods as Amy drapes a wet cloth over his forehead. "Your body temperature is really high, so we're working to bring that down for you, okay? You're going to do great, Colton."

She nods and some of the staff members leave the room. Amy stares at a clock on the wall and shakes her head, hurrying into the hall. She reappears a minute later with ice packs, which she gently places around Colton's neck and armpits. "Hey, Colton? I'm going to slide this along your groin, okay?" Amy's gentle as she works, using a tone of voice I've not seen from her before. This is an entirely different Amy—professional and capable; caring and so, so competent. She explains to him that she's trying to bring down his temperature to help his heart slow down while we wait for the doctor to come in.

I'm not sure whether hours pass or just a few minutes, but eventually I notice everyone has left the room apart from Amy, who continues to murmur soothing words to Colton as she monitors his IV and changes out the ice packs. Finally, a doctor comes in and declares that Colton's in good hands.

"Heat exhaustion," Dr. Manidis says, squeezing Colton's foot since he's got IVs in both arms. "We're going to get you re-hydrated, cooled down, and you'll be on your way, kiddo." She smiles warmly at Colton and Amy and notices me standing in the room. She frowns at me. "Are you Dad?"

My eyes bulge. "Dad? No!"

Colton coughs. "That's my English teacher. Can I call my grandma, though?"

"Of course," I tell him, fishing my phone out of my pocket. "I'm not sure where your stuff got to, but you call home and I'll check in with the school to see where your things are, okay?"

He nods and accepts my phone gingerly, clearly unused to the restrictions of an IV line. "How long do I have to keep these in?"

Dr. Manidis looks up at the IV pole. "I want to do at least two bags of fluids for you and assess your vitals. Should be an hour? Does that seem right, Amy?"

I meet her eye as she nods her agreement with Dr. Manidis's prognosis. "Heart rate's coming down pretty quickly. Things are looking good."

The doctor claps Amy on the back. "You're looking good, too, Peterson. How long until you upgrade?"

Amy swallows and her eyes dart away from mine. She shrugs. Colton hands me my phone and says his grandmother is catching a ride to the hospital to pick him up. Amy smiles at him. "I'll leave you two to talk," she says, gathering up excess materials and organizing them on the cart she rolled into the room.

She backs into the hall and I toss my phone back to Colton. "Hang on to that for me. I'll be right back, okay?" He shrugs and starts scrolling through my apps as I chase after Amy into the hall.

"Amy!" She doesn't stop, rolling the cart toward wherever she needs to go to return the supplies. "Amy, wait!"

CHAPTER SEVEN

Amy

If I don't turn around, I won't have to face him. I won't have to look into his face as he tells me I've blown my chance, missed the final opportunity to pass this class.

I also won't have to think about the inappropriate feelings I got seeing him come in with his student, how calm and collected he was telling Colton everything would be okay. So often, the patients and caregivers in the emergency department are frantic. Screaming, even. Doug was ice cool telling Colton he was in the right place.

I found myself daydreaming about Doug squeezing my own hand and taking care of me sometime.

"Amy!" I hear his deep baritone echo down the hallway as I hurry to the supply closet to return things and clean up a bit. After all, I do need to get out of here if I have any hope of making it to Doug's class this evening. I wonder if he'll be going, since he's here with Colton. Discharge takes forever...

"Amy, can you stop a minute?" I look up to see a hairy hand on the wall by my head and I can feel his presence behind me, warm heat at my back in the chilly hall. I swallow and turn around, meeting his dark eyes. He doesn't have his glasses on today.

I shouldn't be looking at his eyes or taking note of his long lashes. Why do men have long lashes? I don't often make time to spruce myself up, but when I do I always have to layer on the mascara. My lashes are stubby.

"Can we talk?" His voice is warm and it melts my walls.

I look over my shoulder and nod, gripping the handle of the cart a little tighter.

"You weren't in class last night." He swallows and I love watching the slide of his Adam's apple along his throat. God, Doogie has a good throat.

I reach up for my own throat before I realize what I'm doing. "I know."

He sighs deeply and sinks against the wall. "Do you want to tell me what happened?" Doug runs a hand through his hair and a sweaty, dark lock drops across his forehead.

"It's work, Doug. It's always work. And nothing will get better at work until I pass your class. Which I can't do because of work."

He waves a hand around and blows out a breath. "We can work something out about the missed time. But is it really work keeping you from coming? Is there something else?"

I bite the side of my lip, not sure what to say. Is there something else? I can't very well tell him that coming to class means me sitting in the back row imagining him cradling me in his arms, whispering that everything will be okay.

I stare at his shirt and shake my head. We stand in silence for a bit and I can smell him—a little sweaty, a little like sunscreen. I squint to read his shirt. "What even is pickleball?"

Doug laughs and the sound starts to thaw my irritation. I've been irritated since the day Mom got sick, so it's not a huge thaw. But a warm breeze at least. His smile is friendly. "It's a long story. But hey." He squeezes my shoulder and then a horrified expression crosses his face and he pulls back his hand. "Let's talk about class. You can finish this, Amy. Your writing is decent."

"Gee, thanks." I roll my eyes. I know I haven't put in top notch effort. I'm just trying to float this one. I might not be trying too hard at even that...

Doug shakes his head. "What's the bare minimum you need to pass? C-plus?"

"Straight C," I tell him, shifting my weight and returning my hands to the safety of the cart handle.

Doug scratches at his stubble. "Listen, if you at least turn in your last two papers, you can get a C, Amy. And, I mean, you have to show up at class."

I cross my arms over my chest. "I don't want your charity."

His eyes bulge and he stuffs his hands in his pockets, shaking his head. "Are you serious? Charity? I think you're incredible, Amy. You're..." He swallows again. "Students like you are why I became a teacher."

I'm not sure what to make of that revelation. I know he doesn't mean my classroom performance. Doug gestures around the hall. "You're here every day in this stressful environment...saving people. You saved Colton. You *saved* him."

Now it's my turn to stuff my hands in my pockets and hunch my shoulders. "Honestly, he wasn't that sick. You could have given him a bunch of Gatorade and he'd have been fine."

"Don't do that." Doug's expression is stern as he leans toward me. "Don't minimize what you do here." He puts his hand on the wall beside my head again and I can feel my own heart start to accelerate as much as that teenager's had.

I get the sense that he might kiss me.

I can't decide what I'll do if he does.

He moves closer, almost imperceptibly so, and I realize what I'm doing. I'm at work, in the hall outside a patient's room, seconds away from plastering my lips all over my first-year comp instructor.

I shake my head. "I have to go."

"Amy, wait."

I hustle away from him, nearly running. "I'll see you in class later. I promise this time."

I leave Doogie—Doug—in the hall as I reset the supplies and get started on paperwork. The floor is oddly quiet as my shift draws to a close and it looks like I'll be able to leave today with plenty of time to actually eat the food my sister packed me before my class.

I head into the locker room to grab my stuff and try to remember if I got splashed with blood or barf today. I think it was a clean shift, so I keep my scrubs on as I roam out into the rare Pittsburgh sunshine. I walk up Fifth Ave a few blocks and plunk in the grass outside the Soldiers and Sailors Memorial to eat my food.

I still don't have a functioning laptop, but Doug said he'll accept my hand-written scrawl if I can't make it to the computer lab. I should be nicer to him. I bite my lip and pull out the folder, looking at this week's assignment, wondering how much I could possibly finish in the next 45 minutes.

For this persuasive essay, I'd like you to write a letter to a specific change maker. This can be an elected official, an administrator from an organization, etc. Your letter should argue for a policy change, offering examples and using specifics.

Well, I don't have to think very long about this one. I immediately think about how different our lives would be if we had universal healthcare, if my parents hadn't had to re-mortgage their home and blow their savings on Mom's treatment. But who's even in charge of that?

I eat the rest of my meal and think about work. I'm never in charge of any of the insurance stuff but I see plenty of people in anguish about costs. Hell, the kid who came in with Doogie was upset about being uninsured. I have to let all those memories go or I'd never sleep at night, thinking about families wrecked by the costs from a broken leg.

I dust off my hands and decide I'll write to the President of the United States. It's not like I'm actually going to send it. I need to put someone's name at the top of the paper. Once I start writing, I can't stop. My hand aches as I scrawl out the realities my family has faced since my mother's diagnosis. My parents have always worked hard. Have always paid their insurance premiums. We aren't the freeloaders I hear old men complaining about in the waiting room. And here I am, working 50 hours a week while going to school full time, helping my father support my three younger siblings.

The church bells start chiming the hour and it startles me. I realize I've been out here past the time when class is supposed to start, so I stop my "essay" mid-thought and rush off to class. Doug said if I turn *something* in I can get the C. It'll have to do.

CHAPTER EIGHT

Doug

I always save Amy's papers for last. I leave them like a reward for myself, feeling like it's a conversation I'm having with her. Reading her writing is almost as good as talking to her in person. Almost.

Dear President of the United States, her persuasive essay begins, making me chuckle. Any amusement at this lofty salutation is quickly replaced by awe as I continue reading. *I'm writing this to you in between my shift as a tech in a busy trauma center and my three-hour night class to finish my BSN degree. I'm 23, taking classes with 18-year-olds long after I should have wrapped up the student portion of my youth. Why? Because of the way this country handles medical expenses.*

Amy goes on to describe her mother's drawn-out battle with cancer and the subsequent financial ruin her family has struggled to stave off. I knew some of this from our previous conversations, surface level things. But this is a whole new insight into her and I'm blown away by the fierce argument she makes for universal healthcare.

The quality of the writing is impeccable. She makes arguments. She cites examples. Yes, she turned it in on notebook paper speckled with condiments, but this is the best persuasive essay I've read of the group.

More than that, it's a window into the whirlwind of emotion she's been battling for the past few years. With universal healthcare, she argues, she could have had a more normal college experience. She'd still be grieving alongside her family, but she'd be able to afford to replace her broken laptop.

I stare at the pages, awed again by the things she's had to overcome. I read through it again, trying to make sure my admiration for her isn't getting in the way of my thoughts on the writing quality. But no, it's a good paper. It's an amazing paper. And she's an amazing person...one who remains off limits.

I feel bereft now that the class is over, because I know I won't see her again unless someone else I know winds up in her emergency department.

I drag my fingers through my hair, for once wishing I didn't live alone, wishing I could talk to someone. I scroll through my phone, stopping at the selfie I took outside the school. Six weeks feels like a lifetime ago. That was the day I met Amy, I remember, all hot and angry at Dr. Blee's office. I zoom in on the photo and see Colton in the background, trying to give me bunny ears.

I stare at his face another minute, happy that I left my previous life for this one.

The next week and change are brutal. And not just because of the workload. My college course wrapped up, my grad classes wrapped up, and I should be out drinking lite beer and whacking pickle balls with the guys. Or anything resembling fun. Instead I sit in my apartment and mope, pining over a woman who isn't mine to miss.

My phone rings, pulling me out of my grading fog. Two more papers and I'm done with summer school ... for three entire weeks before I start as a full-blown, real middle school teacher.

This summer hasn't been easy, but it's cemented my conviction that I love what I'm doing. But I wasn't ready for my attraction to the fierce almost-nurse and what she would teach me about higher education.

The phone keeps ringing. I glance at the caller ID and smile. "Hey, Colton. How you feeling?"

I can hear the joy in my student's voice as he shouts over the music playing in the background. "I'm real good, Mr. Rogers. Hey, my grandma said an *anonymous benefactor* paid for my hospital stay. Imagine that?"

I grin and sink back into my chair. "That's great to hear, Colton."

"That's the kind of shit that happens to people on television. I mean stuff. Sorry."

"No worries, kiddo. School's not in session right now anyway. I'm really glad someone came through for your family."

"Grandma said she was gonna sue Mr. Nesso for the hospital costs. Not sure if she was serious." It sounds like he's begun eating chips or something similarly crunchy in a crinkly wrapper. The thought of food makes my own stomach gurgle, but I love that my teenaged student feels comfortable enough with me to eat while we talk. I'm learning so much about the kind of teacher I want to be.

Not the kind who is attracted to his undergrads...

I clear my throat. "I'm very glad it didn't come to that." I pause, trying to think of a way to change the subject toward more comfortable material. "While I have you, am I going to see you in the Franklin Scholars this fall? You did great with all your work this summer, even with the pickleball mishap. Ms. Vinelli asked me to be the advisor, and I need some members."

"Hm, I don't know about the scholars thing."

"Well, think about it." I stand up and start searching my apartment for food. Coming up empty, I shove my toes into my flip-flops and hunt for my keys so I can walk out and grab something to go. "The field trips will be safer this fall. I promise."

We share a laugh and I'm reminded again that the situation could have been much more serious. As Colton and I hang up, I think about the primary reason he's perfectly fine right now. Amy Peterson.

I've thought about her nearly nonstop. Not only the way I can see her nipples through the damn scrub top she wore to class, but also about the things I overheard her saying in small group discussions when the students talked about the readings I assigned. Amy is full of fierce convictions about healthcare and policy. She's seen a lot of heavy shit through her work in the emergency department, and I think the other budding nurses in class grew to look up to her.

Frankly, it's hot as fuck. She's this hyper-competent woman with all sorts of obstacles, getting shit done. In my family, people never take charge or speak assertively. It's all about snide, passive-aggressive bullying and passing the buck. This Rogers Family Tradition of business moguls...not one of them could hold Amy Peterson's attention for an instant.

She took all my lesson plans and blew them up in my face this summer. I'll never approach a course prep the same way again, making assumptions about my students. I've thought more than once about what might happen since I submitted final grades. The idea of not seeing her ever again rattles me more than the reality of how inappropriate it is for me to lust after her in this way.

I walk to Chipotle and grab a burrito to go, and while I wait for my food, I refresh my university email to see if my grade rosters are ready for final approval. I've got an email from the registrar, so I pull up the student information software on my phone.

I blow a raspberry and it echoes through the restaurant. She and I agreed on a C, but her writing was much better than average. I chuckle, knowing she'd probably come stab me if I gave her anything higher. She'd accuse me of charity. I'm one click away from entering that C and exiting her from my life. I won't even have her university email address to contact her once she graduates.

When I click approve, I get a ping that this student has fulfilled all graduation requirements and will earn her degree.

"Hot damn," I mutter. "Good for you."

CHAPTER NINE

Amy

I smile at my sleepy-looking sister as she hands me my lunch bag before work. "You didn't have to get up this early, Alice. I am capable of packing my own food."

She shrugs. "It's kind of the least I can do for you. Besides, this one's a special lunch!" When I make a confused face, she claps her hands. "Your first day as a grad nurse, right?"

"Oh." Is it weird I already forgot about my change in status? I worked for so long to get here, it sort of feels anticlimactic. There is a nursing shortage, as always, and my supervisor confirmed with the university that I completed the requirements to graduate, so I get to just work as a grad nurse now while I study for my licensing exams. "I haven't even seen my grades yet. The whole thing is sort of surreal..."

Alice beams. "Well, there's something special in there for you all the same. Don't share it. Just eat it and enjoy. Plus, since you're finally going to have a reasonable schedule, I'm making a fancy dinner this weekend. No arguments!"

I snap my lips shut. I had been primed to protest. We're barely past a point where onions were a splurge. This isn't the time to be buying fancy food. "Only if you get discount ingredients," I chide as I slide the lunch bag into my backpack. It will indeed be strange working a regular schedule, no pressure to pick up additional shifts...no classes...no staring at Doug Rogers.

The last week of class we talked about nurses unions. We were doing more informational essays, and Doug talked us through some published stuff about the impact of unions on healthcare and patient outcomes. It was the sexiest thing I ever experienced in my entire life. This starchy man with his shirt sleeves rolled up, getting passionate about labor unions. My dad would definitely approve.

Not that my dad was ever going to meet my comp teacher.

Anyway, that's all done with now. I walk to the corner in time to wave down the 71B bus toward Oakland, grateful that I catch it early before all the nine to five commuters cram on the route. I take a seat near the front and peek inside my lunch bag, feeling a strange combination of guilt and gratitude when I see the lemon raspberry tart my sister hid inside a reused yogurt container. My sister missed out on a lot of childhood, but even through the grief and hard times, she seems to have maintained her sunshine temperament. I'm glad for that. If someone had to become the bitter old shrew, let it be me. I sniff the dessert and close the lid, excited to eat it later.

When the bus stops on Fifth Avenue near the hospital, I climb off and trudge up the hill toward my entrance. Almost as soon as I'm clocked in, we get a car crash victim and I'm responsible for the blood. When I hear Dr. Manidis shout "mass transfusion," I look at my supervisor. "Four packed red blood cells, four fresh frozen plasma, and 2 platelets, right?"

She gives a thumbs up and nods her head, letting me operate the equipment on my own while she dives in to help with the patient's other needs. The world fades away apart from me, the bags of O negative, and the transfusion machine. This is it, what I worked for all that time. I'm here, doing the work I always wanted to do. And I find myself wanting to tell Doug about it.

I want to see the side of his mouth hitch up in a grin, want to hear what sort of dumb joke he'd make or what fancy news article he'd bring up related to blood bank shortages. I can't wallow in those thoughts now. I've got a job to do.

By the time we get the guy stable, my adrenaline has me twitching. Not bad for my first day.

I steal a half hour to eat my lunch and turn on my phone to check in on my family. Dad says I shouldn't feel like I need to do this, but I honestly don't mind that my siblings come to me with their issues.

I think it's much better than them shutting down or ignoring their problems.

I smile at the congratulations text from my sister and then feel a little sadness that I don't have any emails or anything from Doug. No end of semester wrap-up or checking in about my grade. No thinly veiled, sneaky delivery of his cell so I can call him if I ever need anything.

I set my phone down on the cafeteria table and dig into my special dessert from my sister. From the table beside me, I overhear some of the staff complaining about paperwork and insurance. Nothing new there. We get a lot of irate people calling in to the nurses' station about their bill, even though we have nothing to do with coding or adjusting their debt.

It does mean we know more than we should about who owes what, and how much it really costs someone to break a leg. My ears perk up when I hear Colton's name come up, though. I hadn't realized there was a payment issue with the teen Doug brought in for heat stroke.

"I swear, Carla, it was the strangest phone call I ever got since I started here." The woman from the main information desk leans forward, squeezing a soda can that crinkles as she shares her story. I stare into my dessert so it's a little less obvious that I'm eavesdropping. "The boy's teacher told me he wanted to cover the bill anonymously."

Carla snorts. "Seriously?"

Soda-woman makes an "mmmhmmmm" sound. "Teacher-man paid it himself. Handled the whole thing." She snaps her fingers and Carla gasps. "I hear Maureen from billing at least gave him the self-pay rate."

"I'd hope so," Carla scoffs. "Man, I never had a teacher like that growing up."

"Right? What school's he at? I want to enroll my kid there." They start chatting about their teenagers and I exhale a breath I didn't know I was holding. The plastic fork snaps in my hand as I try to make sense of what I just heard.

Did Doug handle his student's hospital bill personally? It's not totally unreasonable to think the school would pick up the bill for an injury or sickness that happened on their watch... Maybe they sent Doug in to handle it before the kid's parents made it a lawsuit situation?

I fire off an email to Doug asking him to please call me immediately, and then I realize I'm not going to be available immediately. I'm still at work, at the job I worked so hard to obtain. I quickly shove my bag back in my locker and head back out onto the floor to assist with another patient crisis.

The second shift nurses arrive before I have a second to think, and my shift is over. Once I turn my phone back on, I see Doug hasn't emailed me back. I bite my lip, unsure what to do next. I don't even know how to reach him apart from email. I have to know if he did that amazing thing for his student.

Where did he say he works? Did he tell me?

I close my eyes and try to remember the day Doug and Colton came to the hospital. Doug had on a stupid shirt that said something about pickles. Colton had a green shirt with the school name on it...what was it? Fred something...Franklin!

I check the map and see Franklin Middle School is an easy bus ride from here, and the 67 bus turns out to be luxuriously empty even during the afternoon rush. I sprawl out, wondering if I've lost my marbles under the stress of the past few years. Am I really embarking on a cross-town journey to see if my T.A. is a hero?

And what if he is? Do I turn around and get back on the bus after he confirms what I overheard? I don't want that. I want it to be true, and I want him to have done it because of what I wrote in his class. I know that sounds selfish and ridiculous, but I want to know that I affected Doug Rogers somehow, the way he affected me.

I arrive at the school and the place is a ghost town. "Of course, Amy, you idiot. It's summer." I actually have no idea how summer school works, but based on the silent school building, it's not happening here. Not today, anyway. I lean against a column outside the entrance to the school, trying to figure out my next move. Maybe there's a secretary inside or something.

Once I make up my mind that I've come this far and need to locate Doug, I see a guy come out the front of the school carrying a stack of cardboard boxes. He's wearing the same red shirt Doug had on at the E.R.

The pickle shirt.

I rush up behind him. "Excuse me?"

He whips his head around and grins. "You are excused!"

I roll my eyes. "Do you happen to know Doug Rogers?"

The guy drops the boxes on the ground and I see the top one is full of jump ropes. "I do indeed. Please tell me he turned you down romantically, because I would love to white knight this situation and be the happily ever after guy..."

I tuck my sweaty hair behind my ears and make a face at him. "Hardly. I just need to know where he is."

The guy thinks for a minute, shakes his head, and bends over to fish around in the cardboard box, pulling out a sticky note and a pencil. He scribbles something down on it and holds out the note. "Please tell him Newman sent you. I'm going to pry after this. Whatever this is." He gestures between me and the sticky note.

"Nothing to pry about. I just need to clear up a misunderstanding." I tuck the note into the pocket of my scrub top. "Thank you for your help."

"I'm still going to pry."

I wave to him as I head back down the street.

CHAPTER TEN

Doug

I've got to get an air conditioner. As soon as I get my next paycheck, I'm asking Newman for a ride to Costco and buying an air conditioner. I can't keep sitting sprawled on my couch in my ratty basketball shorts chewing ice cubes I took from the machine in the school cafeteria.

Granted, I spent the entire morning hauling boxes around the school. I'd probably be hot and gross even with an A/C. But it'd be a lot nicer to come home to a room without this humidity.

I gnaw on my melting ice and think about my day. I got my classroom all ready to go, with the heavy-ass textbooks organized into stacks for my incoming students. I even helped Newman change out the nets on the basketball hoops in the gym.

I feel like I'm really settling in at Franklin Middle School. Kellie Vinelli's morning memos, dripping with positivity and exclamation points, are even starting to feel comforting. Things are turning out pretty great for me these days, between having my own classroom, acing my first set of grad classes, and scoring a hot pepper rating on that professor rating website. I'd say I hope Amy is the one who gave me that rating, but I somehow doubt she took the time to go online and share her thoughts about my class.

Dr. Blee seemed pretty pleased with the course I taught for the nursing students. I wonder what he'd say if I asked him for Amy's contact information now that she graduated. I snort at the thought of doing that, and nearly choke on an ice cube.

Rattling the remaining ice in my plastic souvenir cup from school, I watch my cell dance across the hardwood floor by my foot. I see that it's my brother calling, which means Mom and Dad are exasperated. I'll call them back in a few days. It's not really any of their business that I sold a chunk of stock to pay for Colton's hospital bill. It's my fucking stock. Or, it was.

Apparently I still have plenty of it left, according to the finance guy who evidently blabbed to them about my private business dealings. Maybe they're calling to yell at me for firing him...I chomp down another ice cube as a reminder to find a new money person to help me. Maybe it'll be Colton someday.

I like the thought of that, of him graduating with a clean slate and going on to do whatever the hell he wants. Isn't that why I'm here, in this sweaty apartment, finishing up summer school *and* summer university teaching?

A knock at my door startles me out of my thoughts about my career path. Forgetting that I'm barefoot and shirtless, I stride over to the door and pull it open. And then I nearly drop my cup of ice when I see Amy Peterson standing on my welcome mat.

She's got her hands on her hips. "Did you pay for that kid's hospital bill?"

I'm so startled to see her that I just freeze, staring.

She snaps her fingers at me. "Doug? Hello? What did you do?"

Confused, I peer down at her and shrug. "What are you doing here? How did you find me?"

She huffs. "Seriously, Rogers. I need to know."

She needs to know, eh? I never intended on telling anyone I footed Colton's bills. I did it because it was the right thing to do. It seems like Amy was checking up on me...thinking about me even after the semester has ended. I feel a pulse of confidence that this woman who awes me might actually want me, too.

I lean against the door jamb and try to cross my arms, yelping when the cold cup of ice comes in contact with my ribs. "I don't know if that's any of your business."

She shakes her head and pushes past me into my apartment, where she proceeds to drop her bag and start pacing in angry circles. "I don't even know why I came over here. I must look like a frazzled mess. Do you know I went to your work to find you? I had to ask someone for directions to your apartment!"

"Amy." I push off the door frame and close the door so the neighbors don't hear her shrieking at me. "Do you have any idea how impactful your writing is?" She puts her hands on her hips and glowers at me. I sigh and run a hand through my sweaty hair. "Look, your insurance essay was the most inspired, most effective piece of writing from the entire batch. You wrote about your mom without sentimentality. You made cutting arguments." I swallow and take a sip of the melted ice water. "It inspired me."

I feel a giant lump form in my throat as I wait for her to make the next move. The air all but leaves the room, seeps out under the door along with my dignity. I stare at her.

Amy's face moves. Her eyes squint and return to normal and she shifts her weight from foot to foot. "I don't know what to do with that."

I exhale through my nose and look into her eyes. "I've wanted you from the first minute I saw you. Your righteous indignation turns me the fuck on. And I couldn't have you, Amy. But I also couldn't just be the same complacent guy I was before. I had to *do* something, because knowing you...inspired me." I feel my bones sag as I wait for her to respond, to react in some way. Amy bites her lip and furrows her brow and stares at me in silence for a few beats.

I open my mouth to mutter something else, but she leaps across the room and shoves me back against the door. I actually do drop the cup in surprise and screech when the cold water splashes on my bare feet. She pushes her hands into my chest, staring up at me. Her breath is an inch away from my face, sweet and hot. I can see her neck moving as her heart beats.

"Doug Rogers," she hisses at me. "Did you pay for that kid's hospital bill?"

I nod my head, just slightly. She's so close to me I can smell her, the heat of her. I nod again and then Amy Peterson stretches up on tiptoes as she yanks my head down toward hers. I feel her palm around the back of my neck as she hauls my face down to her own and she kisses me.

CHAPTER ELEVEN

Amy

"Did you pay for that kid's hospital bill?" I mean for the question to sound sexy. I'm so overcome by his admission that he's attracted to me, that I'm not alone in my complicated feelings about him.

As if I wasn't into him before, he just confirmed that he did in fact use his own damn money to pay for his student's hospital bill like some sort of bespectacled hero.

I realize my hands are pressed against his bare chest. He's blazing hot, his skin so smooth under my skin, moving with his breath. I can feel his heart racing. Doug nods his head and my last shred of restraint melts away. I kiss him.

No. I maul him.

I ram my tongue into his mouth like I'm scolding him, and he returns the move with a delicious moan. Doug drops his water cup and twitches in my arms, and I press closer against him, yanking on his neck as I deepen the kiss.

I can feel the heat of him through my scrub top, seeping into my skin. I'm always perpetually cold at work and I crave his warmth like a lizard needs sunshine. Doug slides his arms around me and I feel functional for the first time in ages. Like I've been sleeping and his body just woke me up.

Eventually, he breaks the kiss, gasping for breath, his palms pressing into my waist as his forehead drops to mine. "Amy," he breathes. I can smell him everywhere, salty and hot and a little dusty. Like an old book. He reaches one hand up to smooth my hair, pressing the locks back from my eyes as my hands continue to explore his skin.

"This is okay, right?" I pull myself closer to him, pressing him harder against the wall in the process. And I feel the length of him against my stomach. All he's wearing is a pair of mesh shorts and we both look down to where his body has already voted on this question.

He swallows and I stare at his throat. I watch the muscles move, see his neck tighten and relax. I trace along his Adam's apple with my finger.

"This is more than okay." He shakes his head. "I never imagined you'd want me, too."

I kiss him again, pulsing my hands against his shoulders to communicate my need before I bite his lip. "You had me at the patient ratio essay," I whisper, and then I melt into the sound of his deep laugh.

Doug moans into my mouth again, his fingers exploring the waist of my scrub pants. My nipples are hard. They're perpetually hard when I'm cold, but now I'm aroused and they pucker against Doug's chest. I need more friction, more of his touch. Just more. "Doug." I break away and kiss his shoulder. "I need a bed."

He grins and stoops to pick up the cup he dropped on the ground. He takes a swig of whatever's inside and tugs me through a doorway into his room. He snaps on a fan by the bed and backs me toward the mattress, where I sink into the sheets that smell like him. I wonder if he's ever lain here and thought of me.

As Doug eases me onto my back, he licks along my collar bone, his tongue freezing cold from the ice in his cup. "Oh!" The contrasting temperatures send my nerves firing like mad as I'm surrounded by his hot body, but focused on his darting, cold tongue.

"I wanted you from the day I heard you yelling at Dr. Blee," he says, thrusting his hips against mine. "I was there. In the hall. Knowing I had to have you."

I moan when his hand finally finds my nipple beneath my top and I squirm to let him lift my shirt up and over my head. "Amy, you light me on fire." Doug shifts his weight to his forearms and I wriggle out of my pants. Beneath him in just my bra and panties, I luxuriate in his heat.

"Good." I nip at his skin. "I'm always cold."

I'm not sure how he gets me out of my underwear or when he loses his shorts, but I finally wrap my hand around his hard length, feeling it stiffen, impossibly hot and hard.

Doug slides a finger between my legs and my knees fall open, letting him in, desperate for more. "Oh, god, you're so wet." He bends his dark head to suck at my nipples and I marvel at his skillful licks.

I've been asleep, physically, for a long time. Just sort of functioning through business and grief and stress. Now I'm coming alive for Doug Rogers, like he's peeling off layers of pain and detachment to wake me up, his altruism and empathy like shock paddles for my emotions.

I wrap my fist around him and tug, loving the moans he makes at my touch. When I reach down to cup his balls he groans and stiffens above me. "Condom," he mutters, stretching over me to the rickety table by his platform bed. He fishes around in the drawer and I tickle his armpit, laughing when he yelps.

Doug sits up on the bed and makes a face at me as he waves the condom packet in the air. "I should torture you. Make you wait for this."

"Don't you dare." I shake my head and try to get my hair out of the way, back over my shoulder. It's no use as the entire mess has come undone.

"Hmm." Doug sets the condom next to my head and, spotting his water glass, chuckles. He reaches into the glass and holds up what's left of a glistening ice cube.

I gasp when I feel it against my nipple. He smiles at me as he circles the tip of my breast with the cube, following the chill with the warmth of his tongue before moving to the other side. "Is that good?"

"So good." I grunt and dig my fingers into his back as he teases me. I watch, impossibly aroused, as the ice melts between his thumb and forefinger and then I shriek when he inserts those chilly digits inside me.

"I'll warm you up," he whispers into my ear, stroking me, petting me until I'm churning beneath him and tangling the sheets. When Doug presses the cold pad of his thumb against my clit, I'm so surprised by the sensation that I scream, coming hard, pulsing around the finger he left inside me.

"Oh, oh, oh," I pant as my hips buck and when I stare into his eyes, his expression is so reverent, dripping with so much yearning that I almost come again. "Doug!"

He nods and reaches for the condom, rolling it on quickly before settling himself between my legs again. I feel the hot tip of him pressing into me and I exhale as he slides inside.

"Fuck, Amy, you're so tight." He shifts his hips, just a little, and I am filled with Doug Rogers. I want to give him every inch of myself, to melt in his heat and his passion and see myself reflected in the look on his face right now.

"You feel so good, Doug." I spread my legs a little wider, and he starts to move, kissing me as he thrusts faster, deeper, pausing with each stroke to grind against my body. The friction is exquisite.

My nails dig into his back as we move together. I love the sounds of our moans, of my name on his lips. I love the challenge of him, the way he isn't intimidated by my harsh words or my anger. He tugs on my hair and I gasp, knowing he sees me. He seems to know what my body needs, a combination of sting with the bliss to unlock my endorphins.

"Doug, I'm going to come again." I pant as he grinds against my clit with each stroke. I dig my heels into his ass cheeks and grunt with the pressure, the building sensations.

"Do it, Amy. Come on my cock."

At the sound of those filthy words from his lips, I do as I'm told. I spasm around him, shaking and moaning until I feel him stiffen and join me in my release.

CHAPTER TWELVE

Doug

"Did that really happen?" I run my fingers through her hair as we lie entwined in my bed, staring into the darkened room as the fan blows across our sweaty bodies.

"It definitely did." She stretches her arms above her head and I smile at her breasts as they move closer to my face with her movements. I want to bury my face in between them and fall asleep surrounded by her softness, with her creamy skin all around me. I want to always be here like this, to soothe away the sting of her anger—help her unwind when she's frustrated.

"I was worried I'd never see you again." I pepper kisses along her temple, growing used to the way she feels in my arms, accepting that she actually is here in my bed. "I was trying to come up with schemes to find you at the hospital."

"No need to stage an emergency, Doogie. I came to you."

"Doogie?"

Amy shrugs. "I decided I was going to call you that on the first day of class. Back when I was still irritated at having to take it."

"Oh, you're done being irritated?" I grin and roll to my side, resting my head on my fist.

She shakes her head. "I'm afraid I'll always be irritated at something."

I pick up one of her hands and weave her fingers together with mine. "I dig your passion." I kiss her hand. "It always seems justified."

"I try." She squeezes my hand and smiles.

Eventually I get up to deal with the condom and return to find her nestled under the blankets. "It's like 85 degrees in here and you're under the covers?"

"They were just here," she mutters. "Calling to me!"

"Come here." I climb in and pull her against my side. "Tell me about your family."

I play with her hair while she describes her sister and her two brothers, how they all still live at home with their dad. How they've all worked together since her mother got sick and passed. They've been through hell, and even though Amy makes fun of her brothers, I can tell she loves them. That they all choose each other.

"I guess you'll have to meet them," Amy declares, like it's a foregone conclusion. She sits up and starts fixing her ponytail, working her fingers through her long locks until I'm hard again. I lie back with my hands crossed behind my neck and she stares. "Well, you're awfully proud of yourself about that."

I nod and pat my lap. "Come back over here and I'll whisper sweet nothings into your ear." Amy laughs, but she does climb onto my lap. And the words I whisper aren't sweet.

"What comes next?" Amy's feet dangle from my couch, her legs bare beneath the pickleball t-shirt she stole from my dresser. Both of us decided we'd rather splurge on delivery than leave the apartment, so she texted her family while I ordered in.

I scratch at my stubble as I wait by the door for the food. "Well, personally, I'd like to eat and then bang you on my couch." She rolls her eyes at me. I laugh. "Next, we figure out your work schedule and we go kayaking or something."

"Kayaking?"

I shrug. "If you'd rather rent a scooter I'm fine with that. I just want to hang out with you, Amy Peterson."

She smiles quietly. There's a knock at the door and I open it a crack to pay the delivery gal, closing the door before anyone can peek at my partially-clothed guest. Amy watches me set out the containers and she sighs. "I don't know how to date someone."

I stuff an egg roll in my mouth and chew a bit before answering. "So don't date me. Just come to my place and yell at me every few days."

"That simple?"

"Some things are simple, Amy." I drop a kiss to her temple and hand her the container of dumplings. She takes one and we eat together in silence for a bit, leaning into each other on the couch. "I still can't believe you're actually here."

"It's weird being here, not worrying about someone's emergency or trying to calm the chaos at home." Amy sets her plate down and sinks back into the couch, eyes closed, hands resting on her stomach. "I love my family so much, but I don't think I ever get to just sit in relative silence."

I reach for her hair, running my fingers through the strands, loving the sensation and the closeness. "I'm glad I can be a recharge for you. You can storm into my apartment any time."

She smiles, not opening her eyes. "I'll hold you to that."

As I watch her fall asleep in my arms, I hope she does.

Epilogue: Doug

I adjust my tie and squint up at the house number. I've been standing on the front porch for long enough that I'm worried I went to the wrong house. I've been with Amy long enough to know that she doesn't look at her phone while she's at work, so I'm assuming she's running late from her shift in the ER.

Just when I'm about to sit down on the step and wait, the front door opens and a young man backs out of the house. "Thank you again, Mr. Peterson." The guy has a stern look about him, and his eyes seem older than his years.

A balding man who must be Amy's father shakes his head. "I want to apologize about that again, Timber. I should never have let that get away from me like that. It's been a year since you mowed the grass for that money."

The young man shrugs and slides his hands in his pockets. "Please don't worry about it. I wouldn't have asked, only I need the money for my brother's hockey fees..."

Bob Peterson—it has to be him—smiles. "You don't have to tell me how the world works, son. You take care now."

The young man nods curtly and walks down the street. It's strange that he didn't acknowledge me standing here, but I suppose it's possible he didn't see me in the shadow. I clear my throat.

Bob turns and his face brightens in the porch light. "Ah! You must be Amy's young man."

I hold out my hand for a shake and Bob returns the gesture, then pulls me in for a hug, startling me. "Any man who wins over my oldest pumpkin gets a hug. C'mere."

I stand in his embrace for a few seconds before I hear a commotion from inside the house. We both turn to look in the door, and I see a woman who looks like Amy, but with wildly curly hair. She's shrieking above a pair of dudes who seem to be in her way as she attempts to strain pasta water in the kitchen. Bob grins. "Should we go in there?"

I raise my eyebrows. "Is it safe?"

He claps me on the back. "You're going to fit into this family just fine, son. Do you like baseball?"

I follow him to the couch as he shouts into the kitchen melee. "Quiet now! Amy's fella is here and we're watching the game."

The curly-haired woman, who must be Alice, pops her head up from the stove. "Oooh, are you Doug? I mean, of course you're Doug. I hope you're hungry." She grins. It looks like she's feeding an army and from the smell of things, the food will be amazing.

I sit on the couch and am soon pressed against Amy's two brothers—one is shouting at his family to quiet down so he can hear the commentator; the other is moaning that he thinks he broke his wrist. "Why didn't you pick her up from work? Then we could eat sooner."

"Ryan!" Bob swats his son with the remote. "Doug doesn't have a car. Amy said that."

"What kind of man doesn't have a car?"

"You," Alice shouts. "You don't have a car, Ry."

They bicker for a few beats and the door flies open. Amy bursts inside, blowing her hair up out of her face. "Oh, god, you're here already," she groans, looking at her watch. "Of course you are. I'm so late."

She walks over to the couch and shoves her brothers away so she can fit beside me. She startles me by pulling me in for a kiss until her brothers start pretending to gag. Amy smiles and the rest of the world melts away. Being with her has felt effortless. She's short-tempered and sharp and it takes all of my wit to keep up with her, and I love every second of it.

I love telling her about my students and hearing about her patients, even the ones who come in with lacerations and broken teeth. I love the ways we are both working to make the world a better place as best as we can.

"Do you hate my family?" She bites her lip as she rubs my hand, as if her family isn't sitting around us on the sofa, listening.

"What, them?" I hook a thumb over my shoulder toward Ryan and Dan. "They're great." And I mean it. Amy's family is real and honest, flawed and warm. "I love them."

"We're right here, kiss-ass." Ryan mutters about having to look up the score of the ballgame later since we're all being so loud.

I lean close to Amy. "I love them," I repeat. And then I realize something that's been building since the day I first set eyes on her. Amy Peterson wasn't part of my lesson plans. I laid out that map without knowing the reality of the terrain ahead. Amy showed up just when I needed help to change course. She's the true compass keeping me on track, missing star I didn't know I had to follow until I saw her huff into my classroom last summer. "And I love you."

Amy smiles at me, her eyes a little teary. "You're okay I guess." She whispers this as her family shouts at some impressive action on the television screen. I rest my palm on her thigh and squeeze. She closes her eyes and then looks up at me again. I wince. "No," she says, with a shake of her head. "I do love you, Doogie."

I lean in and kiss her until her father swats me with the remote.

Want to see more of Doug and Amy?

Doug appears as AJ's best friend in ***Fireball: An Enemies to Lovers Romance***; Amy plays a big role as Alice's sister in ***Sweet Distraction***

Turn the page for a sample chapter for these related books.

Sweet Distraction

ALICE

I parallel park my tiny Honda Civic in the space in front of our house, leaving the driveway for my sister Amy's minivan. These days, it's pretty unusual for adult children to stay living with their parents like this, but the Peterson family loves being together. The four of us kids have stuck together even more since Mom died.

My Dad still owns the giant house where we grew up. He converted the third floor into an apartment when my sister got married and told them to stay until they got their feet under them. They've got a separate entrance and everything. She and her husband have pretty good jobs—she's a nurse and he's a teacher like our mother was—but it's hard to let go of having family so close.

I spend a *lot* of time watching her kids while she's at work. Between me and my brother Dan, my sister never has to use daycare. I guess that's going to change now that I've landed myself such a cool job. I pull my arms to my chest and hug myself, reminding myself that this *is* all real and not some fantasy I dreamed up.

I grab the bags of groceries from the back and pick up the growlers of beer. I practically dance inside and shout to Dan that I'm home and I'm making wings.

"Sweet! That must mean you got the gig, hey sis?" Dan is a year older than me, but he still lives with Dad, too. He sells commercial appliances, and he really knows his stuff. As I cook, I fill him in on the renovation and assure him I'll be placing an order as soon as Dad gets the bid sent over. Between our dad working in construction, my brother Ryan working as a mechanic, and my sister working as a nurse, there isn't much we need to look for outside our immediate family. Dad's brother's an electrician, and one of his sons is a plumber, so we've got our bases covered. My family all looks out for each other, and I wouldn't have it any other way.

Amy comes floating in the door with my nephews. She pecks my cheek as she pours a glass of beer. She takes a sip and her eyes go wide. "This is really good, Al. What is this?"

"Undead Unicorn," I tell her. "It'll go great with the wings if you can wait ten minutes and not drink it all." I flick her with a dishtowel I've got slung over my shoulder and tell my siblings about my new job. "I have complete independence over all of it," I gush. "Whatever I want to cook. I'm my own boss. Sort of. I mean I guess Mr. Stag is my boss-boss, but he told me to do what I think is best."

"Mr. Stag?" My brother teases me, but my sister raises an eyebrow.

"Which Stag?" she asks. "We went to high school with them."

I shake my head. "I never went to school with anyone named Stag. I'd remember them, trust me. But my boss is Tim."

She sighs. "Ah, Tim Stag. Do you know his full name is Timber?"

She runs for the bookshelves in the living room where my dad has kept every book we've ever owned. She slides out her old yearbook. Amy is the oldest, so I guess that would put her around my boss's age. "Here," she says, sliding the book across the counter.

There he is glaring up from the page, looking as intense then as he did today. Dark hair, unreadable grey eyes. Chiseled jaw line. "That's him," I say.

"Timber Stag," my brother chimes in. "Who names their kid Timber?"

Amy flips the pages and we find Thatcher Stag in my brother Ryan's year. "I swear there was another one," she says. "Maybe he went to a magnet school or something? Anyway, spill it, Al. Does he still look this good?"

I nod and tell her about wanting to jump his bones in the kitchen. "Gross, Alice. Come on!" my brother feigns disgust and leaves the room with his beer, but Amy leans across the counter while I finish making dinner.

"And Aim, he smells ah-maze-ing. Not that I spent all day sniffing him, but I caught a whiff. And it was nice."

She nods, looking dreamily at the picture. "He was always sort of standoffish in school. Super serious. I remember him just always being...intense."

"He'd have to be, to build such a successful law practice at his age. Everyone at the office is super driven." I start to tell her about meeting the staff at lunch. "Oh! The third brother is Ty. He plays hockey. My new friend Juniper is going to be his attorney. She was telling me how she was excited that Tim assigned her to be his brother's new lawyer."

My sister laughs when I tell her Juniper suggested I try crew. She pulls out her phone and looks up the rowing team here in Pittsburgh. "Look how fit everyone is," Amy says. "Maybe you should sign up to make them lunch after their workout."

"Very funny, Aim. I'll have you know I keep in shape chasing your sons around." I pause then, remembering that I'm not going to be able to watch them during the day anymore. "Speaking of, we're going to have to talk about my schedule." I start to carry the platters of food to the table as the back door opens and my dad walks in to the kitchen.

"There's my pumpkin patch," says Dad as my nephews swarm around his legs. He plants a kiss on each of us. Amy texts her husband, Doug, to come down for dinner. The seven of us dig in and I smile, thinking how fortunate I am.

Dad and I talk about the renovation and how something like that should only take a few weeks if he lights the right fire under his crew. "Which I will, Pumpkin, don't you worry about that." He tells me that as soon as he can get permits in place, he can get started. "If budget really is no issue, that is," he winks.

My brother and my nephews begin bickering about the newest Ninjago movie and I just feel so content looking around at my family. Our lives are so different now than they might have been if my mother hadn't gotten sick. But even as she was dying, she always told us we needed to stick together, to help each other.

I'm reminded again how I'm leaving my sister high and dry for childcare. I hadn't been expecting the job to begin right away, and I know it's not so easy to just find two daycare spaces with no notice. "Hey Aim," I say, whispering across the table. "What will you do with Ethan and Eli? Mr. Stag was pretty serious about me starting right away."

She furrows her brow. "Well, I don't work again until Friday. That gives me a few days to make calls. Honestly, Al, I don't want you to worry about it. I knew you'd be job hunting when you finished school. I really should have had a plan in place by now." Her husband, Doug, starts helping us brainstorm stopgap childcare options until they can find a place for the boys. They wonder aloud if he should cancel his commitment to teach summer school, but Amy shakes her head.

"Really, it's only for a few more months," she says. "Ethan starts kindergarten in the fall. God, I can't believe he's going to school already."

As they all start to reminisce about my precocious older nephew, my mind slips back to my new job and all the recipes I want to put in place. If I really work hard this week, I'm pretty sure I can get to where I'll be mostly in my office on Friday except for serving and cleaning up lunch. "Hey, Aim, I bet I can bring the boys with me on Friday," I tell her. "I'll just be doing admin stuff by then and they can play in my office when I'm serving lunch."

She looks at me with a severe sort of scowl.

"What?" I say. "They were desperate to have me there. I'll just let someone know I might have the boys this one time."

She frowns, and says, "I somehow can't see Tim Stag feeling excited about a pair of rambunctious boys running around his law firm, Alice. How about we save that for a last resort."

Nodding, I start to clean up, thoughts of meals for the staff racing through my mind.

Continue reading Sweet Distraction, Stag Brothers Book 1 wherever books are sold!

Fireball: An Enemies to Lovers Romance

AJ

By the time I swing through the teacher's lounge to grab my lunch, I've nearly forgotten that Samantha Vine interrupted my class this morning. I definitely am not trying to identify the unique blend of aromatics she uses in her cosmetics and I am absolutely not picturing her each time I bring up gonads with my students.

I will admit to being even more of a growling beast than usual when I see Doug leaning against the refrigerator, smirking at me.

"Had a visitor this morning?" He slurps his PM coffee like a man who doesn't care if it keeps him up past midnight.

"You brought her up to my classroom? In the middle of first period?"

"I did, yes." *Slurp.*

"Come on, Doug. There are protocols for these things. Does she even have clearances? Did you at least take her by the office?"

Slurp.

"Why are you like this?"

He sets the coffee mug on the counter and steps away from the fridge door so I can lean in and snatch my lunch. I yank the bag free and slam myself down into the rickety chair next to the photocopier. Doug slowly crunches a carrot, the sound of his chewing seeming to echo off the floor. Finally, he squints at me. "AJ. Are you suggesting I should have left the CEO of a wealthy tech company—who has tried to offer some financial support to our public school students—on a hard, uncomfortable chair in the office?"

"Yes!" I fling my hands out to the side, but bang my elbow against the copier in the process. I should have just kept my stuff under my desk and eaten my warm lunch alone in my classroom, where I could scroll through online cat videos in peace.

Doug shakes his head. "She said she is the CEO of Vinea, and I know for a fact you were there the other day to ask them to sponsor a field trip. And, as a member of the English department, I would have enjoyed a silent day here at the school, alone with my thoughts, if our students got to embark upon a scientific adventure."

I make a sound at him, one my colleagues have often described as a growl. "I'll find you a famous author your students can visit instead," I tell him, taking a huge bite of my sandwich. Cold meatloaf on white bread. Bubbie's finest. Delicious.

Doug snorts out a laugh. "Yes, because you run in the same social circles with famous authors." When I flip him the bird, Doug points a finger at me. "You know my wife's sister Alice married a Stag. And you also know Emma and Thatcher Stag do a writing and glass-blowing workshop with the kids every winter. We've got the arts all settled."

I actually forgot Doug's wife had that link with local celebrities. I could continue arguing with him just to prove a point, but I don't want to be petty. "Look, Doug, she implied our students aren't qualified to visit her precious space with her fancy coffee and there's no way I'm ever setting these kids up to feel less-than."

He arches a brow at me. "What did she say?"

I try to recall her exact words, and when I can't, Doug jumps in again. "She came here in person to apologize. The CEO of a company in the middle of some very public business dealings. That means something, AJ." He shrugs and rinses his coffee mug before tucking it under his arm along with the remains of the bag of carrots. "Return her call. Let her woo the kids."

He walks out of the room just as two fellow science teachers bustle in. I nod my head at my colleagues as I continue eating my sandwich. Leo slaps a worksheet on the copier and then turns to look at me, smirking even more annoyingly than Doug. "Heard you had a visitor." He waggles his eyebrows.

"This is exactly like middle school," I mutter around a mouthful of sandwich.

Heather laughs as she waits her turn for the copier. "Duh, AJ. But seriously, who the hell scares off a community partner looking to sponsor a field trip? I heard her say she'd even pay for bussing."

I roll my eyes. "There's no way you heard her say that in the middle of a class change."

"Oh I heard it." She points one tawny finger at me. "You know damn well this school has to scrimp to provide soap in the washrooms. Why would you deny these kids a flipping field trip with career exploration opportunities? Go back to your hidey hole right now and call her back before the bell."

I sigh and set down my sandwich. "What exactly am I supposed to say to her?" I truly am hoping Leo and Heather have suggestions because when I think of talking to Samantha Vine, nothing remotely P-G comes to mind. And I can't set myself up for that sort of thing. Not anymore.

Heather rolls her eyes and holds up her hand, pretending it's a phone. In a mock deep voice, she says, "Hello? Ms. Vine? Yes, I can't stop thinking about your offer and I'd be delighted to take you up on it. If you could just put me in touch with your admin team, we can coordinate the details post haste." She mimes hanging up an old-school phone.

"Post haste?"

Leo taps his photocopies on the counter to straighten them and then hits me over the head with the stack as Heather steps up to the copier. "Come on, dude. Grow up. She apologized. She offered the kids a treat." He leans back and studies me. "Is that a new sweater vest?"

I nod and tug at my collar.

Leo nods his approval and Heather starts chanting, "Call her now. Call her now."

Eventually, I hurry out of the room just to get away from their meddling. They're right, of course. Everything about the Vinea building suggested that Samantha is a person who considers the needs of others. Whatever she said yesterday that set me off was likely more about me being sensitive than her being malicious.

And I am sensitive. Maybe I've always been, but definitely since my last breakup. I believe the phrase Leo uses is "frayed nerve." He keeps suggesting I see someone professionally. He's probably right.

I lock the door to my classroom and pull out my phone, scrolling through to my missed calls. I clear my throat and tug at my collar again as I hit the green phone icon. She picks up after 2 rings. *Shit.*

"Excuse me?"

"Did I say that out loud?"

"Is this AJ? Mr. T?"

I clear my throat. "Yes. Hi. Hello. I'm sorry I swore at you. I thought it would go to voicemail."

She laughs and I hate how much I enjoy the sound of it. "Well now we don't have to play phone tag. What's up?" It's like her voice strikes some sort of perfect frequency that lines up the cells in my body. Nope. This will not do.

"I, uh, well, thank you for your offer to treat the students to an in-depth tour of your facilities. And to provide transportation."

"Oooh, are you saying yes? This is terrific." I hear a clicking sound and imaging her typing a rapid email off to an underling while we speak. Must be nice to have underlings...although there are enough people in my life reminding me I could have underlings, too, if I hadn't chosen a life of "servitude." "What sort of time frame were you thinking?"

"I, uh, wasn't quite expecting us to work through the logistics right this minute." My collar seems to be shrinking in the afternoon heat. I keep pulling it away from my wind pipe.

"Hmm, well I'd like to settle as many details as possible right now to avoid unnecessary back and forth. Much more efficient if we just hash it out, right?" She doesn't give me time to respond. "You'll need time for permission slips and such, right? So let's look two weeks out. That's mid-September. How's the 17th?"

I shake my head. "No school that day. For Rosh Hashanah."

"Oh, really? It's late this year."

"You're familiar with Rosh Hashanah timing?" I'm not accustomed to people like Samantha knowing about Jewish traditions. I expected her to respond with some inane question about matzah. If I'm honest, I was hoping I'd get to tell her she had her holidays mixed up. It's much easier for me if the women I'm attracted to show me their flaws right up front, so I know not to get attached.

She continues talking. "Mm hm. Lots of my employees use their flex holidays in September for the Days of Awe. Okay, well, how about Wednesday of that week?"

Days of Awe. This woman knows the lingo of my people. I gulp. "I guess that's fine."

"Wonderful! And how many students do you have?"

By the time Samantha Vine is done, I've agreed to let her team "craft" the permission form to include questions about dietary restrictions and access needs, and she vows to send a courier with printed forms by the end of the school day so we can distribute them at dismissal. She practically sings me off the phone and hangs up, leaving me staring at the phone in my hand as my fifth period students start jiggling the knob of my classroom door.

Continue reading Fireball: An Enemies to Lovers Romance wherever books are sold!

www.ingramcontent.com/pod-product-compliance
Lightning Source LLC
LaVergne TN
LVHW050942080826
845145LV00004B/1378

* 9 7 8 1 9 5 7 1 4 5 1 8 1 *